Dear Reader,

Welcome to the world of Stephanie Plum!

When I first created Stephanie, I had no idea how many people would relate to her. Now, she's kind of taken the world by storm (and taken over my life!). Back when she was just a figment of my imagination, I wanted to create a character who could kick butt, but still be human; who could appreciate the finer points of fugitive apprehension, as well as the finer points of the food court at the mall.

Here's a sampler of some of my favorite scenes from the Stephanie Plum novels. If you've never read these books before, I hope you get a kick out of them. And if you're a Stephanie Plum fan, you'll recognize some of the wildest, wackiest, most hilarious moments from the books—complete with Stephanie's loveable, dysfunctional family: her long-suffering mother, her even longer-suffering father, Grandma Mazur, and of course, her Perfect Sister Valerie.

And I can't help but mention the two men in her life: Ranger (her mentor and tormentor) and Joe Morelli, the sexiest vice cop this side of the Jersey Turnpike.

People often ask me why my novels are so popular. I think it's because the world of Stephanie Plum is a world you recognize—except in technicolor and going eighty miles per hour! Am I Stephanie Plum? No, but I have a very good idea where she lives.

So enjoy, happy reading, and if you're ever in Trenton, New Jersey, don't forget to visit Pino's Pizza or the Tasty Pastry. . . .

Best wishes,

Janet Evanovich

Take a trip down the Jersey Turnpike—

where life is more unpredictable than you can imagine.

Save $3.00 with this special mail-in rebate offer on Janet Evanovich's new hardcover, *To The Nines*— available July 15, 2003

#1 *NEW YORK TIMES*
BESTSELLING AUTHOR

JANET EVANOVICH

Invites you to discover the world of Stephanie Plum . . .

St. Martin's Paperbacks

ISBN: 0-312-99434-6

Printed in the United States of America

St. Martin's Paperbacks edition / June 2003

St. Martin's Paperbacks are published by St. Martin's Press, 175 Fifth Avenue, New York, NY 10010.

10 9 8 7 6 5 4 3 2 1

CONTENTS

Laugh-out-loud scenes from:

ONE FOR THE MONEY	1
TWO FOR THE DOUGH	4
THREE TO GET DEADLY	7
FOUR TO SCORE	10
HIGH FIVE	11
HOT SIX	13
SEVEN UP	15

Excerpt from:

HARD EIGHT	16

A special sneak preview from:

TO THE NINES	29

Plumography—Guide to the world of Plum 45

EXCERPT FROM
ONE FOR THE MONEY

Grandma Mazur glared out at Bernie. "Who are you?"

"I'm Bernie Kuntz."

"What do you want?"

I looked the length of the hall, and I could see Bernie shift uncomfortably on his feet.

"I've been invited for dinner," Bernie said.

Grandma Mazur still had the screen door shut. "Helen," she yelled over her shoulder, "there's a young man at the door. He says he's invited to dinner. Why didn't someone tell me about this? Look at this old dress I'm wearing. I can't entertain a man in this dress."

I'd known Bernie since he was five. I'd gone to grade school with Bernie. We ate lunch together in grades one through three, and I would forever associate him with peanut butter and jelly on Wonder bread. I'd lost touch with him in high school. I knew he'd gone to college, and that after college he'd gone to work selling appliances in his father's store.

He was medium height, with a medium build that had never lost its baby fat. He was all dressed up in shiny tassel loafers, dress slacks, and sports coat. So far as I could see, he hadn't changed much since sixth grade. He looked like he still couldn't add fractions, and the little metal pull on his zipper was sticking out, creating a tiny tent with his fly.

We took our seats at the table and concentrated on the business of eating.

"Bernie sells appliances," my mother said, passing the red cabbage. "He makes good money at it, too. He drives a Bonneville."

"A Bonneville. Imagine that," Grandma Mazur said.

My father kept his head bent over his chicken. He rooted for the Mets, he wore Fruit of the Loom underwear, and he drove a Buick. His loyalties were carved in stone, and he wasn't about to be impressed by some upstart of a toaster salesman who drove a Bonneville.

Bernie turned to me. "So what are you doing now?"

I fiddled with my fork. My day hadn't exactly been a success, and announcing to the world that I was a fugitive apprehension agent seemed presumptuous. "I sort of work for an insurance company," I told him.

"You mean like a claims adjuster?"

"More like collections."

"She's a bounty hunter!" Grandma Mazur announced. "She tracks down dirty rotten fugitives just like on television. She's got a gun and everything." She reached behind her to the sideboard, where I'd left my shoulder bag. "She's got a whole pocketbook full of paraphernalia," Grandma Mazur said, setting my bag on her lap. She pulled out the cuffs, the beeper, and a travel pack of tampons and set them on the table. "And here's her gun," she said proudly. "Isn't it a beauty?"

I have to admit it was a pretty cool gun. It had a stainless steel frame and carved wood grips. It was a Smith and Wesson 5-shot revolver, Model 60. A .38 Special. Easy to use, easy to carry, Ranger had said. And it had been much more reasonable than a semi-automatic, if you can call $400 reasonable.

"My God," my mother shouted, "put it away! Someone take the gun from her before she kills herself!"

The cylinder was open and clearly empty of rounds. I didn't know much about guns, but I knew this one couldn't go bang without bullets. "It's empty," I said. "There are no bullets in it."

Grandma Mazur had both hands wrapped around the gun with her finger on the trigger. She scrinched an eye closed and sighted on the china closet. "Ka-pow," she said. "Ka-pow, ka-pow, ka-pow."

My father was busy with the sausage dressing, studiously ignoring all of us.

"I don't like guns at the table," my mother said. "And the dinner's getting cold. I'll have to reheat the gravy."

"This gun won't do you no good if you don't have bullets in it," Grandma Mazur said to me. "How're you gonna catch those killers without bullets in your gun?"

Bernie had been sitting openmouthed through all of this. "Killers?"

"She's after Joe Morelli," Grandma Mazur told him. "He's a bona fide killer and a bail dodger. He plugged Ziggy Kulesza right in the head."

"I knew Ziggy Kulesza," Bernie said. "I sold him a big-screen TV about a year ago. We don't sell many big screens. Too expensive."

"He buy anything else from you?" I asked. "Anything recent?"

"Nope. But I'd see him sometimes across the street at Sal's Butcher Shop. Ziggy seemed okay. Just a regular sort of person, you know?"

No one had been paying attention to Grandma Mazur. She was still playing with the gun, aiming and sighting, getting used to the heft of it. I realized there was a box of ammo beside the tampons. A scary thought skittered into my mind. "Grandma, you didn't load the gun, did you?"

"Well of course I loaded the gun," she said. "And I left the one hole empty like I saw on television. That way you can't shoot nothing by mistake." She cocked the gun to demonstrate the safety of her action. There was a loud bang, a flash erupted from the gun barrel, and the chicken carcass jumped on its plate.

"Holy mother of God!" my mother shrieked, leaping to her feet, knocking her chair over.

"Dang," Grandma said, "guess I left the wrong hole empty." She leaned forward to examine her handiwork. "Not bad for my first time with a gun. I shot that sucker right in the gumpy."

My father had a white-knuckle grip on his fork, and his face was cranberry red.

I scurried around the table and carefully took the gun from Grandma Mazur. I shook out the bullets and shoveled all my stuff back into my shoulder bag.

"Look at that broken plate," my mother said. "It was part of the set. How will I ever replace it?" She moved the plate, and we all stared in silence at the neat round hole in the tablecloth and the bullet embedded in the mahogany table.

Grandma Mazur was the first to speak. "That shooting gave me an appetite," she said. "Somebody pass me the potatoes."

EXCERPT FROM TWO FOR THE DOUGH

I flipped the light switch and closed the door behind me. I dumped my pocketbook and new shoes on the kitchen counter and jumped back with a yelp when the phone rang. Too much excitement for one day, I told myself. I was on overload.

"How about now?" the caller said. "Are you scared now? Have I got you thinking?"

My heart missed a beat. "Kenny?"

"Did you get my message?"

"What message are you talking about?"

"I left a message for you in your jacket pocket. It's for you and your new buddy, Spiro."

"Where are you?"

The disconnect clicked in my ear.

Shit.

I plunged my hand into my jacket pocket and started pulling stuff out . . . used Kleenex, lipstick, a quarter, a Snickers wrapper, a dead finger. "YOW!"

I dropped everything on the floor and ran out of the room. "Shit, damn, shit!" I stumbled into the bathroom and stuck my head into the toilet to throw up. After a few minutes I decided I wasn't going to throw up (which was kind of too bad since it'd be good to get rid of the hot fudge sundae I'd had with Mary Lou).

I washed my hands with a lot of soap and hot water and crept back to the kitchen. The finger was lying in the middle of the floor. It looked very embalmed. I snatched at the phone, staying as far away from the finger as was humanly possible, and dialed Morelli.

"Get over here," I said.

"Something wrong?"

"JUST GET OVER HERE!"

Ten minutes later the elevator doors opened and Morelli stepped out.

"Uh-oh," he said, "the fact that you're waiting for me in the hall is probably not a good sign." He looked at my apartment door. "You don't have a dead body in there, do you?"

"Not entirely."

"You want to enlarge on that?"

"I have a dead finger on my kitchen floor."

"Is the finger attached to anything? Like a hand or an arm?"

"It's just a finger. I think it belongs to George Mayer."

"You recognized it?"

"No. It's just that I know George is missing one. You see, Mrs. Mayer was going on about George's lodge, and how he wanted to be buried with his ring, and so Grandma had to check the ring out, and in the process broke off one of

George's fingers. Turns out the finger was wax. Somehow Kenny got into the mortuary this morning, left Spiro a note, and chopped off George's finger. And then while I was at the mall tonight with Mary Lou, Kenny threatened me in the shoe department. That must have been when he put the finger in my pocket."

"Have you been drinking?"

I gave him a don't-be-stupid look and pointed to my kitchen.

Morelli moved past me and stood hands on hips, staring down at the finger on the floor. "You're right. It's a finger."

"When I came in tonight the phone was ringing. It was Kenny, telling me he left a message in my jacket pocket."

"And the message was the finger."

"Yeah."

"How did it get on the floor?"

"It sort of dropped there when I went to the bathroom to throw up."

Morelli helped himself to a paper towel and used it to pick up the finger. I gave him a plastic bag, he dropped the finger in, sealed the bag, and slipped the bag into his jacket pocket. He leaned against the kitchen counter and crossed his arms over his chest. "Let's start from the beginning."

EXCERPT FROM

THREE TO GET DEADLY

I dropped Lula at the office and went home to check my messages and my bank account. There were no messages, and I had a few dollars left in checking. I was almost current on my bills. My rent was paid for the month. If I continued to mooch meals from my mother I could afford highlights. I studied myself in the mirror, fluffing my hair, imagining a radiant new color. "Go for it," I said to myself. Especially since the alternative was to dwell on Leroy Watkins.

I locked up and drove to the mall, where I persuaded Mr. Alexander to work me into his schedule. Forty-five minutes later I was under the dryer with my hair soaked in chemical foam, wrapped in fifty-two squares of aluminum foil. Stephanie Plum, space creature. I was trying to read a magazine, but my eyes kept watering from the heat and fumes. I dabbed at my eyes and looked out through the wide-open arch door and plate-glass windows into the mall.

It was Saturday, and the mall was crowded. Passersby glanced my way. Their stares were emotionless. Empty curiosity. Mothers and children. Kids hanging out. Stuart Baggett. *Holy cow!* It was that little twerp Stuart Baggett at the mall!

Our eyes met and held for a moment. Recognition registered. Stuart mouthed my name and took off. I flipped the dryer hood back and came out of the seat like I was shot from a cannon.

We were on the lower level, sprinting toward Sears. Stuart had a good head start and hit the escalator running. He was pushing people out of his way, apologizing profusely, looking charmingly cute.

I jumped onto the escalator and elbowed my way forward, closing ground. A woman with shopping bags belligerently stood in front of me.

"Excuse me," I said. "I need to get through."

"I got a right to be on this escalator," she said. "You think you own this place?"

"I'm after that kid!"

"You're a kook, that's what you are. Help!" she yelled. "This woman is crazy! This is a crazy woman."

Stuart was off the escalator, moving back down the mall. I held my breath and danced in place, keeping him in view. Twenty seconds later I was off the stairs, running full tilt with the foil flapping against my head, the brown beauty parlor smock still tied at the waist.

Suddenly Stuart was gone, lost in the crowd. I slowed to a walk, scanning ahead, checking side stores. I jogged through Macy's. Scarves, sportswear, cosmetics, shoes. I reached the exit and peered out into the parking lot. No sign of Stuart.

I caught myself in a mirror and stopped dead. I looked like Flypaper Woman meets Alcoa Aluminum. Foilhead does Quaker Bridge Mall. If I saw anyone I knew while I looked like this I'd drop dead on the spot.

I had to pass back through Macy's to get to the mall, including a foray through cosmetics where I might encounter Joyce Barnhardt, queen of the makeover. And after Macy's I still had to negotiate the escalator and main corridor of the mall. This was not something I wanted to do in my present condition.

I'd left my shoulder bag at the beauty parlor, so purchasing a scarf was out of the question. I could rip out the little foil squares wrapped around my hair, but I'd paid sixty dollars to have the squares put on.

I took another look in the mirror. Okay, so I was getting my hair done. What's the big deal? I raised my chin a fraction of an inch. Belligerent. I'd seen my mother and grandmother take this stance a million times. There's no better defense than a steely-eyed offense.

I briskly walked the length of the store and turned to the escalator. A few people stared, but most kept their eyes firmly averted.

Mr. Alexander was pacing at the entrance to the salon. He was looking up and down the mall, and he was muttering. He saw me, and he rolled his eyes.

Mr. Alexander always wore black. His long hair was slicked back in a ducktail. His feet were clad in black patent leather loafers. Gold cross earrings dangled from his earlobes. When he rolled his eyes he pinched his lips together.

"Where did you go?" he demanded.

"After a bail jumper," I said. "Unfortunately, I lost him."

Mr. Alexander tugged a foil packet off my head. "Unfortunately, you should have had your head in the rinse bowl ten minutes ago! That's unfortunate." He waved his hand at one of his underlings. "Miss Plum is done," he said. "We need to rinse her immediately." He removed another foil and rolled his eyes. "Unh," he said.

"What?"

"I'm not responsible for this," Mr. Alexander said.

"What? What?"

Mr. Alexander waved his hand again. "It will be fine," he said. "A little more spectacular than we'd originally imagined."

Spectacular was good, right? I held that thought through the rinse and the comb-out.

"This will be wonderful once you get used to it," Mr. Alexander said from behind a cloud of hair spray.

I squinted into the mirror. My hair was orange. Okay, don't panic. It was probably the lights. "It looks orange," I told Mr. Alexander.

"California sun-kissed," Mr. Alexander said.

I got out of the chair and took a closer look. "My hair is orange!" I shouted. "It's freaking ORANGE!"

EXCERPT FROM
FOUR TO SCORE

Morelli nudged my knee with his. "Want to go for a ride?"

Of course I wanted to go for a ride. I was dying to get my legs around those 109 horses and feel them wind out.

"Do I get to drive?" I asked.

"No."

"Why not?"

"It's *my* bike."

"If I had a Ducati, I'd let *you* drive."

"If you had a Ducati you probably wouldn't talk to a lowlife like me."

"Remember when I was six and you were eight, and you conned me into playing choo-choo in your father's garage?"

Morelli's eyes narrowed. "We aren't going to go through this again, are we?"

"I never got to be the train. *You* were always the train. *I* always had to be the tunnel."

"I had better train equipment."

"You owe me."

"I was eight years old!"

"What about when I was sixteen, and you seduced me behind the eclair case at the bakery?"

"What about it?"

"I never got the top. I was only the bottom."

"This is entirely different."

"This is no different! This is the same thing!"

"Jesus," Morelli said. "Just get on the damn bike."

"You're going to let me drive, right?"

"Yeah, you're going to drive."

I ran my hand over the bike. It was sleek and smooth and red.

Morelli had a second helmet strapped to the backseat. He unhooked the cord and gave me the helmet. "Seems a shame to cover up all those pretty curls."

I buckled on the helmet. "Too late for flattery."

It had been a while since I'd driven a bike. I settled myself onto the Duc and looked things over.

Morelli took the seat behind me. "You know how to drive this, right?"

I revved the engine. "Right."

"And you have a license?"

"Got a bike license when I was married to Dickie. I've kept it current."

He held me at the waist. "This is going to even the score."

"Not nearly."

"Entirely," he said. "In fact, this ride's going to be so good you're going to owe *me* when it's done."

Oh boy.

EXCERPT FROM
HIGH FIVE

I was in the lobby, waiting for Ranger at six o'clock. I was all showered and perfumed and hair freshly done up to look sexily unkempt. Mike's Place is a sports bar frequented by businessmen. At six o'clock it would be filled with suits catching ESPN and having a drink to unwind before going home, so I chose to look suity, too. I was wearing my Wonderbra, which worked wonders, a white silk shirt unbuttoned clear to the front clasp on the magical bra, and a black silk suit with the skirt rolled at the waist to show a lot of leg. I covered the mess at the waist with a wide fake leopard skin belt, and I stuffed my stocking-clad feet into four-inch fuck-me pumps.

Mr. Morganthal shuffled out of the elevator and winked at me. "Hey, hootchie-mamma," he said. "Want a hot date?" He was ninety-two and lived on the third floor, next to Mrs. Delgado.

"You're too late," I told him. "I've already made plans."

"That's just as well. You'd probably kill me," Mr. Morganthal said.

Ranger pulled up in the Mercedes, and idled at the door. I gave Mr. Morganthal a tweak on the cheek and sashayed out, swinging my hips, wetting my lips. I poured myself into the Mercedes and crossed my legs.

Ranger looked at me and smiled. "I told you to get his attention . . . not start a riot. Maybe you should button one more button."

I batted my eyelashes at him, in fake-flirt, which actually wasn't totally fake. "You don't like it?" I said. Hah! Take that, Morelli. Who needs you!

Ranger reached over and flipped the next two buttons open, exposing me to mid-belly. "That's the way *I* like it," he said, the smile still in place.

Shit! I quickly rebuttoned the buttons. "Wise guy," I said. Okay, so he called my bluff. No reason to panic. Just file it away for future reference. *Not ready for Ranger!*

EXCERPT FROM
HOT SIX

Introducing Bob the dog:

Bob was waiting patiently in the car, and he got all happy-looking when we opened the doors and slid in.

"Maybe Bob needs breakfast," Lula said.

"Bob already had breakfast."

"Let me put it another way. Maybe Lula needs breakfast."

"You have anything special in mind?"

"I guess I could use one of those Egg McMuffins. And a vanilla shake. And breakfast fries."

I put the Buick in gear and headed for the drive-through.

"How's it going?" the kid at the window said. "You still looking for a job?"

"I'm thinking about it."

We got three of everything and parked on the edge of the lot to eat and regroup. Bob ate his Egg McMuffin and breakfast fries in one chomp. He slurked his milkshake down and looked longingly out the window.

"Think Bob needs to stretch his legs," Lula said.

I opened the door and let him out. "Don't go far."

Bob jumped out and started walking around in circles, occasionally sniffing the pavement.

"What's he doing?" Lula wanted to know. "Why's he walking in circles? Why's he—Uh-oh, this don't look good. Looks to me like Bob's taking a big poop in the middle of the parking lot. Holy cow, look at that! That's a mountain of poop."

Bob returned to the Buick and sat down, wagging his tail, smiling, waiting to be let back in.

I let him in, and Lula and I slumped down low in our seats.

"Do you think anyone saw?" I asked Lula.

"I think *everyone* saw."

"Damn," I said. "I don't have the pooper-scooper with me."

"Pooper-scooper, hell. I wouldn't go near that with a full contamination suit and a front-loader."

"I can't just leave it there."

"Maybe you could run over it," Lula said. "You know . . . flatten it out."

I cranked the engine over, backed up, and pointed the Buick at the pile of poop.

"Better roll the windows up," Lula said.

"Ready?"

Lula braced herself. "Ready."

I stomped on the gas and took aim.

SQUISH!

We rolled the windows down and looked out.

"So what do you think? You think I should make another pass?"

"Wouldn't hurt," Lula said. "And I'd forget about getting a job here."

EXCERPT FROM
SEVEN UP

"What was that all about?" Lula wanted to know.

"DeChooch has Grandma Mazur. He wants to trade her for the heart. I'm supposed to take the heart to Quaker Bridge Mall, and he's going to call me at seven with further instructions. He said he'll kill her if I bring the police into it."

"Kidnappers always say that," Lula said. "It's in the kidnapper handbook."

"What are you going to do?" Connie wanted to know. "Do you have any idea who has the heart?"

"Hold up here," Lula said. "Louie D don't have his name engraved on his heart. Why don't we just get another heart? How's Eddie DeChooch gonna know if it's Louie D's heart? I bet we could give Eddie DeChooch a cow heart and he wouldn't know. We just go to a butcher and tell him we need a cow heart. We don't go to a butcher in the Burg because word might get around. We go to some other butcher. I know a couple over on Stark Street. Or we could try Price Chopper. They've got a real good meat department.

"I'm surprised DeChooch didn't come up with this. I mean, nobody has even seen Louie D's heart except for DeChooch. And DeChooch can't see for shit. DeChooch probably took that pot roast out of Dougie's freezer thinking it was the heart."

"Lula's come up with something here," Connie said. "It might work."

I picked my head up from between my legs. "It's creepy!"

"Yeah," Lula said. "That's the best part." She looked at

the clock on the wall. "It's lunchtime. Let's go get a burger and then we'll get a heart."

I used Connie's phone to call my mother.

"Don't worry about Grandma," I said. "I know where she is and I'm going to pick her up later tonight." Then I hung up before my mother could ask questions.

EXCERPT FROM
HARD EIGHT

Lately, I've been spending a lot of time rolling on the ground with men who think a stiffy represents personal growth. The rolling around has nothing to do with my sex life. The rolling around is what happens when a bust goes crapola and there's a last ditch effort to hog-tie a big, dumb bad guy possessing a congenitally defective frontal lobe.

My name is Stephanie Plum, and I'm in the fugitive apprehension business . . . bond enforcement, to be exact, working for my cousin Vincent Plum. It wouldn't be such a bad job except the direct result of bond enforcement is usually incarceration—and fugitives tend to not like this. Go figure. To encourage fugitive cooperation on the way back to the pokey I usually persuade the guys I capture to wear handcuffs and leg shackles. This works pretty good most of the time. And, if done right, cuts back on the rolling around on the ground stuff.

Unfortunately, today wasn't most of the time. Martin Paulson, weighing in at 297 pounds and standing five feet, eight inches tall, was arrested for credit card fraud and for being a genuinely obnoxious person. He failed to show for his court appearance last week, and this put Martin on my Most Wanted List. Since Martin is not too bright, he hadn't been too hard to find. Martin had, in fact, been at home engaged in what he does best . . . stealing merchandise off the Internet. I'd managed to get Martin into cuffs and leg shackles and into my car. I'd even managed to drive Martin to the police station on North Clinton Avenue. Unfortunately, when I attempted to get Martin *out* of my car he tipped over and was now rolling around on his belly, trussed up like a Christmas goose, unable to right himself.

We were in the parking lot adjacent to the municipal building. The back door leading to the docket lieutenant was less than fifty feet away. I could call for help, but I'd be the brunt of cop humor for days. I could unlock the cuffs or ankle shackles, but I didn't trust Paulson. He was royally pissed off, red-faced and swearing, making obscene threats and horrifying animal sounds.

I was standing there, watching Paulson struggle, wondering what the hell I was going to do, because anything short of a forklift wasn't going to get Paulson up off the pavement. And just then, Joe Juniak pulled into the lot. Juniak is a former police chief and is now mayor of Trenton. He's a bunch of years older than me and about a foot taller. Juniak's second cousin, Ziggy, is married to my cousin-in-law Gloria Jean. So we're sort of family . . . in a remote way.

The driver's side window slid down, and Juniak grinned at me, cutting his eyes to Paulson. "Is he yours?"

"Yep."

"He's illegally parked. His ass is over the white line."

I toed Paulson, causing him to start rocking again. "He's stuck."

Juniak got out of his car and hauled Paulson up by his armpits. "You don't mind if I embellish this story when I spread it all over town, do you?"

"I do mind! Remember, I voted for you," I said. "And we're almost related."

"Not gonna help you, cutie. Cops live for stuff like this."

"You're not a cop anymore."

"Once a cop, always a cop."

Paulson and I watched Juniak get back into his car and drive away.

"I can't walk in these things," Paulson said, looking down at the shackles. "I'm gonna fall over again. I haven't got a good sense of balance."

"Have you ever heard the bounty hunter slogan, Bring 'em back—dead or alive?"

"Sure."

"Don't tempt me."

Actually, bringing someone back dead is a big no-no, but this seemed like a good time to make an empty threat. It was late afternoon. It was spring. And I wanted to get on with my life. Spending another hour coaxing Paulson to walk across the parking lot wasn't high on my list of favored things to do.

I wanted to be on a beach somewhere with the sun blistering my skin until I looked like a fried pork rind. Okay, truth is at this time of year that might have to be Cancún, and Cancún didn't figure into my budget. Still, the point was, I didn't want to be *here* in this stupid parking lot with Paulson.

"You probably don't even have a gun," Paulson said.

"Hey, give me a break. I haven't got all day for this. I have other things to do."

"Like what?"

"None of your business."

"Hah! You haven't got anything better to do."

I was wearing jeans and a T-shirt and black Caterpillar boots, and I had a real urge to kick him in the back of his leg with my size-seven CAT.

"Tell me," he said.

"I promised my parents I'd be home for dinner at six."

Paulson burst out laughing. "That's pathetic. That's fucking pathetic." The laughter turned into a coughing fit. Paulson leaned forward, wobbled side to side, and fell over. I reached for him, but it was too late. He was back on his belly, doing his beached whale imitation.

. . .

My parents live in a narrow duplex in a chunk of Trenton called the Burg. If the Burg was a food, it would be pasta—penne rigate, ziti, fettuccine, spaghetti, and elbow macaroni, swimming in marinara, cheese sauce, or mayo. Good, dependable, all-occasion food that puts a smile on your face and fat on your butt. The Burg is a solid neighborhood where people buy houses and live in them until death kicks them out. Backyards are used to run a clothesline, store the garbage can, and give the dog a place to poop. No fancy backyard decks and gazebos for Burgers. Burgers sit on their small front porches and cement stoops. The better to see the world go by.

I rolled in just as my mother was pulling the roast chicken out of the oven. My father was already in his seat at the head of the table. He stared straight ahead, eyes glazed, thoughts in limbo, knife and fork in hand. My sister, Valerie, who had recently moved back home after leaving her husband, was at work whipping potatoes in the kitchen. When we were kids Valerie was the perfect daughter. And I was the daughter who stepped in dog poo, sat on gum, and constantly fell off the garage roof in an attempt to fly. As a last ditch effort to preserve her marriage, Valerie had traded in her Italian-Hungarian genes and turned herself into Meg Ryan. The marriage failed, but the blonde Meg-shag persists.

Valerie's kids were at the table with my dad. The nine-year-old, Angie, was sitting primly with her hands folded, resigned to enduring the meal, an almost perfect clone of Valerie at that age. The seven-year-old, Mary Alice, the kid from hell, had two sticks poked into her brown hair.

"What's with the sticks?" I asked.

"They not sticks. They're antlers. I'm a reindeer."

This was a surprise because usually she's a horse.

"How was your day?" Grandma asked me, setting a bowl of green beans on the table. "Did you shoot anybody? Did you capture any bad guys?"

Grandma Mazur moved in with my parents shortly after

Grandpa Mazur took his fat clogged arteries to the all-you-can-eat buffet in the sky. Grandma's in her midseventies and doesn't look a day over ninety. Her body is aging, but her mind seems to be going in the opposite direction. She was wearing white tennis shoes and a lavender polyester warm-up suit. Her steel gray hair was cut short and permed to within an inch of its life. Her nails were painted lavender to match the suit.

"I didn't shoot anybody today," I said, "but I brought in a guy wanted for credit card fraud."

There was a knock at the front door, and Mabel Markowitz stuck her head in and called, "Yoohoo."

My parents live in a two-family duplex. They own the south half, and Mabel Markowitz owns the north half, the house divided by a common wall and years of disagreement over house paint. Out of necessity, Mabel's made thrift a religious experience, getting by on Social Security and government-surplus peanut butter. Her husband, Izzy, was a good man but drank himself into an early grave. Mabel's only daughter died of uterine cancer a year ago. The son-in-law died a month later in a car crash.

All forward progress stopped at the table, and everyone looked to the front door, because in all the years Mabel had lived next door, she'd never once *yoohoo*ed while we were eating.

"I hate to disturb your meal," Mabel said. "I just wanted to ask Stephanie if she'd have a minute to stop over, later. I have a question about this bond business. It's for a friend."

"Sure," I said. "I'll be over after dinner." I imagined it would be a short conversation since everything I knew about bond could be said in two sentences.

Mabel left and Grandma leaned forward, elbows on the table. "I bet that's a lot of hooey about wanting advice for a friend. I bet Mabel's been busted."

Everyone simultaneously rolled their eyes at Grandma.

"Okay then," she said. "Maybe she wants a job. Maybe she wants to be a bounty hunter. You know how she's always squeaking by."

My father shoveled food into his mouth, keeping his head down. He reached for the potatoes and spooned seconds onto his plate. "Christ," he mumbled.

"If there's anyone in that family who would need a bail bond, it would be Mabel's ex-grandson-in-law," my mother said. "He's mixed up with some bad people these days. Evelyn was smart to divorce him."

"Yeah, and that divorce was real nasty," Grandma said to me. "Almost as nasty as yours."

"I set a high standard."

"You were a pip," Grandma said.

My mother did another eye roll. "It was a disgrace."

Mabel Markowitz lives in a museum. She married in 1943 and still has her first table lamp, her first pot, her first chrome-and-Formica kitchen table. Her living room was newly wallpapered in 1957. The flowers have faded but the paste has held. The carpet is dark Oriental. The upholstered pieces sag slightly in the middle, imprinted with asses that have since moved on . . . either to God or Hamilton Township.

Certainly the furniture doesn't bear the imprint of Mabel's ass as Mabel is a walking skeleton who never sits. Mabel bakes and cleans and paces while she talks on the phone. Her eyes are bright, and she laughs easily, slapping her thigh, wiping her hands on her apron. Her hair is thin and gray, cut short and curled. Her face is powdered first thing in the morning to a chalky white. Her lipstick is pink and applied hourly, feathering out into the deep crevices that line her mouth.

"Stephanie," she said, "how nice to see you. Come in. I have a coffee cake."

Mrs. Markowitz *always* has a coffee cake. That's the way it is in the Burg. Windows are clean, cars are big, and there's always a coffee cake.

I took a seat at the kitchen table. "The truth is, I don't

know very much about bond. My cousin Vinnie is the bond expert."

"It's not so much about bond," Mabel said. "It's more about finding someone. And I fibbed about it being for a friend. I was embarrassed. I just don't know how to even begin telling you this."

Mabel's eyes filled with tears. She cut a piece of coffee cake and shoved it into her mouth. Angry. Mabel wasn't the sort of woman to comfortably fall victim to emotion. She washed the coffee cake down with coffee that was strong enough to dissolve a spoon if you let it sit in the cup too long. *Never* accept coffee from Mrs. Markowitz.

"I guess you know Evelyn's marriage didn't work out. She and Steven got a divorce a while back, and it was pretty bitter," Mabel finally said.

Evelyn is Mabel's granddaughter. I've known Evelyn all my life, but we were never close friends. She lived several blocks away, and she went to Catholic school. Our paths only intersected on Sundays when she'd come to dinner at Mabel's house. Valerie and I called her the Giggler because she giggled at everything. She'd come over to play board games in her Sunday clothes, and she'd giggle when she rolled the dice, giggle when she moved her piece, giggle when she lost. She giggled so much she got dimples. And when she got older, she was one of those girls that boys love. Evelyn was all round softness and dimples and vivacious energy.

I hardly ever saw Evelyn anymore, but when I did there wasn't much vivacious energy left in her.

Mabel pressed her thin lips together. "There was so much arguing and hard feelings over the divorce that the judge made Evelyn take out one of these new child custody bonds. I guess he was afraid Evelyn wouldn't let Steven see Annie. Anyway, Evelyn didn't have any money to put up for the bond. Steven took the money that Evelyn got when my daughter died, and he never gave Evelyn anything. Evelyn was like a prisoner in that house on Key Street. I'm almost the only relative left for Evelyn and Annie now, so I put my house here up for collateral. Evelyn wouldn't have gotten custody if I didn't do that."

This was all new to me. I'd never heard of a *custody* bond. The people I tracked down were in violation of a *bail* bond.

Mabel wiped the table clean of crumbs and dumped the crumbs in the sink. Mabel wasn't good at sitting. "It was all just fine until last week when I got a note from Evelyn, saying she and Annie were going away for a while. I didn't think much of it, but all of a sudden everyone is looking for Annie. Steven came to my house a couple days ago, raising his voice and saying terrible things about Evelyn. He said she had no business taking Annie off like she did, taking her away from him and taking her out of first grade. And he said he was invoking the custody bond. And then this morning I got a phone call from the bond company telling me they were going to take my house if I didn't help them get Annie back."

Mabel looked around her kitchen. "I don't know what I'd do without the house. Can they really take it from me?"

"I don't know," I told Mabel. "I've never been involved in anything like this."

"And now they all got me worried. How do I know if Evelyn and Annie are okay? I don't have any way of getting in touch. And it was just a note. It wasn't even like I talked to Evelyn."

Mabel's eyes filled up again, and I was really hoping she wasn't going to flat-out cry because I wasn't great with big displays of emotion. My mother and I expressed affection through veiled compliments about gravy.

"I feel just terrible," Mabel said. "I don't know what to do. I thought maybe you could find Evelyn and talk to her . . . make sure her and Annie are all right. I could put up with losing the house, but I don't want to lose Evelyn and Annie. I've got some money set aside. I don't know how much you charge for this sort of thing."

"I don't charge anything. I'm not a private investigator. I don't take on private cases like this." Hell, I'm not even a very good bounty hunter!

Mabel picked at her apron, tears rolling down her cheeks now. "I don't know who else to ask."

Oh man, I don't believe this. Mabel Markowitz, crying! This was at about the same comfort level as getting a gyno exam in the middle of Main Street at high noon.

"Okay," I said. "I'll see what I can do . . . as a neighbor."

Mabel nodded and wiped her eyes. "I'd appreciate it." She took an envelope from the sideboard. "I have a picture for you. It's Annie and Evelyn. It was taken last year when Annie turned seven. And I wrote Evelyn's address on a piece of paper for you, too. And her car and license plate."

"Do you have a key to her house?"

"No," Mabel said. "She never gave me one."

"Do you have any ideas about where Evelyn might have gone? Anything at all?"

Mabel shook her head. "I can't imagine where she's taken off to. She grew up here in the Burg. Never lived anyplace else. Didn't go away to college. Most all our relatives are right here."

"Did Vinnie write the bond?"

"No. It's some other company. I wrote it down." She reached into her apron pocket and pulled out a folded piece of paper. "It's True Blue Bonds, and the man's name is Les Sebring."

My cousin Vinnie owns Vincent Plum Bail Bonds and runs his business out of a small storefront office on Hamilton Avenue. A while back when I'd been desperate for a job, I'd sort of blackmailed Vinnie into taking me on. The Trenton economy has since improved, and I'm not sure why I'm still working for Vinnie, except that the office is across from a bakery.

Sebring has offices downtown, and his operation makes Vinnie's look like chump change. I've never met Sebring but I've heard stories. He's supposed to be extremely professional. And he's rumored to have legs second only to Tina Turner's.

I gave Mabel an awkward hug, told her I'd look into things for her, and I left.

My mother and my grandmother were waiting for me. They were at my parents' front door with the door cracked an inch, their noses pressed to the glass.

"*Pssst,*" my grandmother said. "Hurry up over here. We're dying."

"I can't tell you," I said.

Both women sucked in air. This went against the code of the Burg. In the Burg, blood was *always* thicker than water. Professional ethics didn't count for much when held up to a juicy piece of gossip among family members.

"Okay," I said, ducking inside. "I might as well tell you. You'll find out anyway." We rationalize a lot in the Burg, too. "When Evelyn got divorced she had to take out something called a child custody bond. Mabel put her house up as collateral. Now Evelyn and Annie are off somewhere, and Mabel is getting pressured by the bond company."

"Oh my goodness," my mother said. "I had no idea."

"Mabel is worried about Evelyn and Annie. Evelyn sent her a note and said she and Annie were going away for a while, but Mabel hasn't heard from them since."

"If I was Mabel I'd be worried about her *house*," Grandma said. "Sounds to me like she could be living in a cardboard box under the railroad bridge."

"I told her I'd help her, but this isn't really my thing. I'm not a private investigator."

"Maybe you could get your friend Ranger to help her," Grandma said. "That might be better anyway, on account of he's hot. I wouldn't mind having him hang around the neighborhood."

Ranger is more associate than friend, although I guess friendship is mixed in there somehow, too. Plus a scary sexual attraction. A few months ago we made a deal that has haunted me. Another one of those jumping-off-the-garage-roof things, except this deal involved my bedroom. Ranger is Cuban-American with skin the color of a mocha latte, heavy on the mocha, and a body that can best be described as *yum.* He's got a big-time stock portfolio, an endless, inexplicable supply of expensive black cars, and skills that make Rambo look like an amateur. I'm pretty sure he only kills bad guys, and I think he might be able to fly like Superman, although the flying part has never been confirmed. Ranger works in bond enforcement, among other things. And Ranger always gets his man.

My black Honda CR-V was parked curbside. Grandma walked me to the car. "Just let me know if there's anything I can do to help," she said. "I always thought I'd make a good detective, on account of I'm so nosy."

"Maybe you could ask around the neighborhood."

"You bet. And I could go to Stiva's tomorrow. Charlie Shleckner is laid out. I hear Stiva did a real good job on him."

New York has Lincoln Center. Florida has Disney World. The Burg has Stiva's Funeral Home. Not only is Stiva's the premier entertainment facility for the Burg, it's also the nerve center of the news network. If you can't get the dirt on someone at Stiva's, then there isn't any dirt to get.

It was still early when I left Mabel's, so I drove past Evelyn's house on Key Street. It was a two-family house very much like my parents'. Small front yard, small front porch, small two-story house. No sign of life in Evelyn's half. No car parked in front. No lights shining behind drawn drapes. According to Grandma Mazur, Evelyn had lived in the house when she'd been married to Steven Soder and had stayed there with Annie when Soder moved out. Eddie Abruzzi owns the property and rents out both units. Abruzzi owns several houses in the Burg and a couple large office buildings in downtown Trenton. I don't know him personally, but I've heard he's not the world's nicest guy.

I parked and walked to Evelyn's front porch. I rapped lightly on her door. No answer. I tried to peek in the front window, but the drapes were drawn tight. I walked around the side of the house and stood on tippy toes, looking in. No luck with the side windows in the front room and dining room, but my snoopiness paid off with the kitchen. No curtains drawn in the kitchen. There were two cereal bowls and two glasses on the counter next to the sink. Everything else seemed tidy. No sign of Evelyn or Annie. I returned to the front and knocked on the neighbor's door.

The door opened, and Carol Nadich looked out at me.

"Stephanie!" she said. "How the hell are you?"

I went to school with Carol. She got a job at the button factory when we graduated and two months later married Lenny Nadich. Once in a while I run into her at Giovichinni's Meat Market, but beyond that we've lost touch.

"I didn't realize you were living here," I said. "I was looking for Evelyn."

Carol did an eye roll. "Everyone's looking for Evelyn. And to tell you the truth, I hope no one finds her. Except for you, of course. Those other jerks I wouldn't wish on anyone."

"What other jerks?"

"Her ex-husband and his friends. And the landlord, Abruzzi, and his goons."

"You and Evelyn were close?"

"As close as anyone could get to Evelyn. We moved here two years ago, before the divorce. She'd spend all day popping pills and then drink herself into a stupor at night."

"What kind of pills?"

"Prescription. For depression, I think. Understandable, since she was married to Soder. Do you know him?"

"Not well." I met Steven Soder for the first time at Evelyn's wedding nine years ago, and I took an instant dislike to him. In my brief dealings with him over the following years I found nothing to change my original bad impression.

"He's a real manipulative bastard. And abusive," Carol said.

"He'd hit her?"

"Not that I know. Just mental abuse. I could hear him yelling at her all the time. Telling her she was stupid. She was kind of heavy, and he used to call her 'the cow.' Then one day he moved out and moved in with some other woman. Joanne Something. Evelyn's lucky day."

"Do you think Evelyn and Annie are safe?"

"God, I hope so. Those two deserve a break."

I looked over at Evelyn's front door. "I don't suppose you have a key?"

Carol shook her head. "Evelyn didn't trust anyone. She was real paranoid. I don't think her grandma even has a key. And she didn't tell me where she was going, if that's your next question. One day she just loaded a bunch of bags into her car and took off."

I gave Carol my card and headed for home. I live in a three-story brick apartment building about ten minutes from the Burg . . . five, if I'm late for dinner and I hit the lights right. The building was constructed at a time when energy was cheap and architecture was inspired by economy. My bathroom is orange and brown, my refrigerator is avocado green, and my windows were born before Thermopane. Fine by me. The rent is reasonable, and the other tenants are okay. Mostly the building is inhabited by seniors on fixed incomes. The seniors are, for the most part, nice people . . . as long as you don't let them get behind the wheel of a car.

I parked in the lot and pushed through the double glass door that led to the small lobby. I was filled with chicken and potatoes and gravy and chocolate layer cake and Mabel's coffee cake, so I bypassed the elevator and took the stairs as penance. All right, so I'm only one flight up, but it's a start, right?

My hamster, Rex, was waiting for me when I opened the door to my apartment. Rex lives in a soup can in a glass aquarium in my kitchen. He stopped running on his wheel when I switched the light on and blinked out at me, whiskers whirring. I like to think it was *welcome home* but probably it was *who put the damn light on?* I gave him a raisin and a small piece of cheese. He stuffed the food into his cheeks and disappeared into his soup can. So much for roommate interaction.

In the past, Rex has sometimes shared his roommate status with a Trenton cop named Joe Morelli. Morelli's two years older than I am, half a foot taller, and his gun is bigger than mine. Morelli started looking up my skirt when I was six, and he's just never gotten out of the habit. We've had some differences of opinion lately, and Morelli's toothbrush is not currently in my bathroom. Unfortunately, it's a lot harder to get Morelli out of my heart and my mind than out of my bathroom. Nevertheless, I'm making an effort.

I got a beer from the fridge and settled in front of the television. I flipped through the stations, hitting the high points, not finding much. I had the photo of Evelyn and Annie in front of me. They were standing together, looking happy. Annie had curly red hair and the pale skin of a natural redhead. Evelyn had her brown hair pulled back. Conservative makeup. She was smiling, but not enough to bring out the dimples.

A mom and her kid . . . and I was supposed to find them.

Special Sneak Preview FROM TO THE NINES

My name is Stephanie Plum, and I was born and raised in the Chambersburg section of Trenton, where men pretty much only drop their drawers in private. Thank God for small favors because the top activities for men in the Burg are scarfing pastries and pork rinds and growing ass hair. The pastry and pork rind scarfing I've seen firsthand. The ass hair growing is for the most part rumor.

The first butt I saw up close and personal belonged to Joe Morelli. Morelli put an end to my virgin status and showed me an ass that was masculine perfection . . . smooth and muscular and blemish-free. Back then Morelli thought a long-term commitment was twenty minutes. I was one of thousands who got to admire Morelli's bare ass as he pulled his pants up and headed for the door.

Morelli's been in and out of my life since then. He's currently *in*, and he's improved with age, butt included.

So the sight of a naked ass isn't exactly new to me, but the one I was presently watching took the cake. Punky Balog had an ass like Winnie the Pooh . . . big and fat and furry. Sad to say, that was where the similarity ended because, unlike Pooh Bear, there was nothing endearing or cuddly about Punky Balog.

I knew about Punky's ass because I was in my new sunshine-yellow Ford Escape, sitting across from Punky's dilapidated row house, and Punky had his huge Pooh butt plastered against his second-story window. My sometimes partner, Lula, was riding shotgun for me, and Lula and I were staring up at the butt in open-mouthed horror.

Punky slid his butt side to side on the pane, and Lula and I gave a collective, upper-lip-curled-back *ee-yeuuw*!

"Think he knows we're out here," Lula said. "Think maybe he's trying to tell us something."

Lula and I work for my bail bonds agent cousin, Vincent Plum. Vinnie's office is on Hamilton Avenue, his front window looking into the Burg. He's not the world's best bonds agent. And he's not the worst. Truth is, he'd probably be a better bondsman if he wasn't saddled with Lula and me. I do fugitive apprehension for Vinnie, and I have a lot more luck than skill. Lula mostly does filing. Lula hasn't got luck *or* skill. The thing Lula has going for her is the ability to tolerate Vinnie. Lula's a plus-size black woman in a size-seven white world, and Lula's had a lot of practice at pulling attitude.

Punky turned and gave us a wave with his johnson.

"That's just so sad," Lula said. "What do men think of? If you had a lumpy little wanger like that, would you go waving it in public?"

Punky was dancing now, jumping around, wanger flopping, doodles bouncing.

"Holy crap," Lula said. "He's gonna rupture something."

"It's gotta be uncomfortable."

"I'm glad we forgot the binoculars. I wouldn't want to see this up close."

I didn't even want to see it from a distance.

"When I was a 'ho, I used to keep myself from getting grossed out by pretending men's privates were Muppets," Lula said. "This guy looks like an anteater Muppet. See the little tuft of hair on the anteater head and then there's the thing the anteater snuffs up ants with . . . Except ol' Punky here's gotta get real close to the ants on account of his snuffer isn't real big. Punky's got a pinky."

Lula was a 'ho in a previous life. One night while plying her trade, she had a near-death experience and decided to change everything but her wardrobe. Not even a near-death experience could get Lula out of spandex. She was currently wearing a skin-tight, hot pink miniskirt and a tiger-print top that made her boobs look like big, round, over-inflated balloons. It was early June and mid-morning and the Jersey air wasn't cooking yet, so Lula had a yellow angora sweater over the tiger top.

"Hold on," Lula said. "I think his snuffer is growing."

This produced another *eeyeuuw* from us.

"Maybe I should shoot him," Lula said.

"No shooting!" I felt the need to discourage Lula from hauling out her Glock, but truth was, it seemed like it'd be a public service to take a potshot at Punky.

"How bad do we want this guy?" Lula asked.

"If I don't bring him in, I don't get paid. If I don't get paid, I don't have rent money. If I don't have rent money, I get kicked out of my apartment and have to move in with my parents."

"So we want him real bad."

"*Real* bad."

"And he's wanted for what?"

"Grand theft auto."

"At least it's not armed robbery. I'm gonna be hoping the only weapon he's got, he's holding in his hand right now . . .

on account of this don't look like much of a threat to me."

"I guess we should go do it."

"I'm ready to rock and roll," Lula said. "I'm ready to kick some Punky butt. I'm ready to do the job."

I turned the key in the ignition. "I'm going to drop you at the corner so you can cut through the back and take the back door. Make sure you have your walkie-talkie on so I can let you know when I'm coming in."

"Roger, that."

"And no shooting, no breaking doors down, no Dirty Harry imitations."

"You can count on me."

Three minutes later, Lula reported she was in place. I parked the Escape two houses down, walked to Punky's front door, and rang the bell. No one responded so I rang a second time. I gave the door a solid rap with my fist and shouted, "Bond enforcement. Open the door!"

I heard shouting carrying over from the backyard, a door crashing open and slamming shut, and then more muffled shouting. I called Lula on the talkie but got no response. A moment later, the front door opened to the house next to me and Lula stomped out.

"Hey, so excuse me," she yelled at the woman behind her. "So I got the wrong door. It could happen, you know. We're under a lot of pressure when we're making these dangerous apprehensions."

The woman glared at Lula, and slammed and locked her door shut.

"Must have miscounted houses," Lula said to me. "I sort of busted in the wrong door."

"You weren't supposed to bust in *any* door."

"Yeah, but I heard someone moving around inside. Guess that's 'cause it was the neighbor lady's house, hunh? So what's going on? How come you're not in yet?"

"He hasn't opened the door."

Lula took a step back and looked up. "That's because he's still mooning you."

I followed Lula's line of sight. She was right. Punky had his ass to the window again.

"Hey," Lula yelled up. "Get your fat ass off the window and get down here. We're trying to do some bond enforcement."

An old man and an old woman came out of the house across the street and settled themselves on their front stoop to watch.

"Are you going to shoot him?" the old man wanted to know.

"I don't hardly ever get allowed to shoot anybody," Lula told him.

"That's darn disappointing," the man said. "How about kicking the door down?"

Lula gave the man one of her hand on hip, *get real* looks. "Kick the door down? Do I look like I could kick a door down in these shoes? These are Via Spigas. You don't go around kicking down doors in Via Spigas. These are classy shoes. I paid a shitload of money for these shoes and I'm not sticking them through some cheap-ass door."

Everyone looked at me. I was wearing jeans, a t-shirt topped by a black jeans jacket, and CAT boots. CAT boots could definitely kick down a door, but they'd have to be on someone else's foot because door kicking was a skill I lacked.

"You girls need to watch more television," the old man said. "You need to be more like those Charlie's Angels. Nothing stopped them girls. They could kick doors down in all kinds of shoes."

"Anyways, you don't need to kick the door in," the old woman said. "Punky never locks it."

I tried the door and sure enough, it was unlocked.

"Sort of takes the fun out of it," Lula said, looking past the door into Punky's house.

This is the part where if we were Charlie's Angels, we'd get into crouched positions, holding our guns in two hands in front of us, and we'd hunt down Punky. Fortunately, we didn't have a camera crew following us around today, because I left my gun home in the cookie jar on my kitchen counter, and Lula'd fall over if she tried to do the crouch thing in her Via Spigas.

"Hey, Punky," I yelled up the stairs, "put some clothes on and come down here. I need to talk to you."

"No way."

"If you don't get down here, I'm going to send Lula up to get you."

Lula's eyes got wide and she mouthed, *Me? Why me?*

"Come up here and get me," Punky said. "I have a surprise for you."

Lula pulled a Glock out of her handbag and gave it over to me. "You should take this on account of *you're* gonna be the one going up the stairs first and you might need it. You know how I hate surprises."

"I don't want the gun. I don't like guns."

"Take the gun."

"I don't want the gun," I told her.

"*Take* the *gun*!"

Yeesh. "Okay, okay. Give me the stupid gun."

I got to the top of the stairs and I peeked around the corner, down the hall.

"Here I come, ready or not," Punky sang out. And then he jumped from behind a bedroom door and stood spread-eagle in full view. "Ta-dahhhh."

He was buck-naked and slick as a greased pig. Lula and I swallowed hard, and we both took a step backward.

"What have you got all over you?" I asked.

"Vaseline. Head to toe and extra heavy in the cracks and crevices." He was smiling ear to ear. "You want to take me in, you have to wrestle with me."

"How about we just shoot you?" Lula said.

"You can't shoot me. I'm not armed."

"Here's the plan," I said to Lula. "We cuff him and put him in leg irons, and then we wrap him in a blanket so he doesn't get my car greasy."

"I'm not touching him," Lula said. "Not only is he an ugly, naked motherfucker, but he's a dry cleaning bill waiting to happen. I'm not ruining this top. I'll never find another top like this. It's genuine fake tiger. And Lord knows what he'd do to rabbit."

I reached for him with the cuffs. "Give me your hand."

"Make me," he said, waggling his butt. "Come get me, sweetie pie."

Lula looked over at me. "You *sure* you don't want me to shoot him?"

I took my jacket off and snatched at his wrist, but I couldn't hold tight. After three attempts, I had Vaseline up to my elbow, and Punky was skipping around going, *Nah, nah, nah, you can't catch me, I'm the gingerbread man.*

"This guy's in the red zone on the Breathalyzer," Lula said. "Think he might also be missing a few marbles in his greased-up jughead."

"I'm smart like a fox," Punky said. "If you can't catch hold of me, you can't take me in. If you can't take me in, I don't go to jail."

"If I don't take you in, I don't pay my rent and I get kicked out of my apartment," I told Punky, lunging for him, swearing when he slid away from me.

"This here's embarrassing," Lula said. "I can't believe you're trying to grab this funky fat man."

"It's my job. And you could help! Take the damn top off if you don't want it to get ruined."

Punky turned away from me; I gave him a good hard kick to the back of his knee, and he crashed to the floor. I threw myself on top of him and yelled to Lula to cuff him. She managed to get both cuffs on, and my cell phone chirped.

It was my Grandma Mazur on the phone. When my Grandpa Mazur cashed in his two-dollar chips and went on to the High Rollers' Room in the Sky, my Grandma Mazur moved in with my parents.

"Your mother's locked herself in the bathroom with the carving knife, and she won't come out," Grandma said. "It's the menopause. Your mother was always so sensible until the menopause hit."

"What on earth is she doing in the bathroom with the carving knife?"

"That's just it . . . she won't tell me. I saw her go up with the knife, and then I heard the door click, and now she won't say nothing. For all I know, she's in the tub with her wrist slit."

"*Omigod.*"

"Anyways, I thought you could get over here and unlock the door like you did last time when your sister locked herself in the bathroom."

My sister Valerie locked herself in the bathroom with a pregnancy test kit . . . not a carving knife. The test kit kept turning up positive, and if I was Valerie, I would have wanted to spend the rest of my life locked in the bathroom too.

"I wasn't the one who unlocked the door," I told Grandma. "I was the one who climbed onto the roof over the back stoop and went in through the window."

"Well, whatever you did, you better get over here and do it again. Your father's off somewhere, and your sister's at work. I'd shoot the lock off, but last time I tried to do that the bullet ricocheted off the doorknob and took out a table lamp."

"Are you sure this is an emergency? I'm sort of in the middle of something."

"Hard to tell what's an emergency in this house anymore."

My parents lived in a small, three-bedroom, one-bathroom house that, was bursting at the scams with my mom and dad, my grandma, my recently divorced, very pregnant sister, and her two kids. Emergencies were beginning to blend with the normal.

"Hang tight," I told Grandma. "I'm not far away. I'll be there in a couple minutes."

Lula looked down at Punky. "What are we gonna do with him?"

"We're going to take him with us."

"The hell you are," Punky said. "I'm not getting up. I'm not going anywhere."

"I don't have time to mess with this," I said to Lula. "You stay here and babysit, and I'll send Vinnie over to do the pickup."

"You're in trouble now," Lula said to Punky. "I bet Vinnie likes greased-up, fat men. People tell me Vinnie used to be romantically involved with a duck. I bet he's gonna think you're just fine."

I hustled down the stairs and out the front door to the Escape. I called Vinnie on the way to my parents' house and gave him the word on Punky.

"What are you, nuts?" Vinnie yelled at me. "I'm not gonna go out to pick up some greased-up, naked guy. I write bonds. I don't do pickups. Read my lips . . . *you're the pickup person.*"

"Fine. Then *you* go to my parents' house and get my knife-wielding mother out of the bathroom."

"Alright, alright, I'll do your pickup, but it's come to a sad state of affairs when I'm the normal member of this family."

I couldn't argue with that one.

Grandma Mazur was waiting for me when I pulled to the curb. "She's still in there," Grandma said. "She won't talk to me or nothing."

I ran up the stairs and tried the door. Locked. I knocked. No answer. I yelled to my mother. Still no response. Damn. I ran down the stairs, out to the garage, and got a stepladder. I put the ladder up to the back stoop and climbed onto the small, shingled roof that attached to the back of the house and gave me access to the bathroom window. I looked inside.

My mom was in the tub with earphones on, eyes closed, knees sticking out of the water like two smooth, pink islands. I rapped on the window, and my mom opened her eyes and gave a shriek. She grabbed for the towel and continued to scream for a good sixty seconds. Finally she blinked, snapped her mouth shut, pointed straight-armed to the bathroom door, and mouthed the word *Go*.

I scuttled off the roof, down the ladder, and slunk back to the house and up the stairs, followed by Grandma Mazur.

My mother was at the bathroom door, wrapped in a towel, waiting. "What the hell were you doing?" she yelled. "You scared the crap out of me. Jesus! Can't I even relax in the tub?"

Grandma Mazur and I were speechless, standing rooted to the spot, our mouths open, our eyes wide. My mom never cursed. My mom was the practical, calming influence on the family. My mom went to church. My mom *never* said crap.

"It's the change," Grandma said.

"It is *not* the change," my mother shouted. "I am *not* menopausal. I just want a half hour alone. Is that too much to ask? A crappy half hour!"

"You brought the knife into the bathroom," Grandma said. "I thought you were going to kill yourself. You wouldn't answer me."

"I bought myself a headset so I could listen to music without disturbing anyone. And then I couldn't get the package open. So I brought a knife up because all the scissors are God-knows-where. And I didn't hear you because I was listening to the music. I just wanted to take a bath, but now that you mention it . . . killing myself doesn't sound like a bad idea."

"I bet you've been reading those women's magazines again," Grandma said. "They're always talking about relaxing in the tub with candles. And then you're supposed to pleasure yourself, but I'm not sure what that means."

"I'm going to get the knife off the toilet," my mother said, her voice eerily calm. "And when I wrap my hand around that knife, both of you better be gone." She leaned forward and took a closer look at my shirt. "What on earth do you have all over you? It's in your hair and on your shirt, and you have big grease stains on your jeans. It looks like . . . Vaseline."

"I was in the middle of a capture when Grandma called."

My mother slapped her hand to her forehead and closed her eyes. "Where did I go wrong? What did I do to deserve this?" she asked. She opened her eyes and gave me serious.

"I don't want to know the details," she said. "I don't *ever* want to know the details."

Ten minutes later I was pushing through the front door to Vinnie's office. Connie Rosolli, Vinnie's office manager and guard dog, was behind her desk, newspaper in hand. Connie was a couple years older than me, an inch or two shorter and had me by three cup sizes. She was wearing a blood-red, v-neck sweater that showed a lot of cleavage. Her nails and her lips matched the sweater.

There were two women occupying the chairs in front of Connie's desk. Both women were dark-skinned and wearing traditional Indian dresses. The older woman was a size up from Lula. Lula is packed solid, like a giant bratwurst. The woman sitting across from Connie was loose flab with rolls of fat cascading between the halter top and the long skirt of her sari. Her black hair was tied in a knot low on her neck and shot with grey. The younger woman was slim and I guessed slightly younger than me. Late twenties, maybe. They both were perched on the edge of their seats, hands tightly clasped in their laps.

"We've got trouble," Connie said to me. "There's an article in the paper today about Vinnie."

"It's not another duck incident, is it?" I asked.

"It's about the visa bond Vinnie wrote for Samuel Singh. Singh is here on a three-month work visa, and Vinnie wrote a bond insuring Singh would leave when his visa was up. A visa bond is a new thing so the paper's making a big deal about it."

Connie handed me the paper, and I looked at the photo accompanying the feature. Two slim, shifty-looking men with slicked-back, black hair, smiling. Singh was from India, his complexion darker, his frame smaller than Vinnie's. Both men looked like they regularly conned old ladies out of their life savings. Two Indian women stood in the background, behind Vinnie and Singh. The women in the photo were the women sitting in front of Connie.

"This is Mrs. Apusenja and her daughter Nonnie," Connie said. "Mrs. Apusenja rented a room to Singh."

"And he's disappeared," Mrs. Apusenja said. "We are very worried."

Oh boy. I skimmed the article. Apusenja's bond was up in a week. If Vinnie couldn't produce Singh in a week's time, he was going to look like an idiot.

"We think something terrible happened to him," the younger woman said. "We think he must be kidnapped. He was a wonderful person. He would never just leave without a word."

The mother nodded in agreement. "Samuel has been staying with us while working in this country. My family is very close to Samuel Singh's family in India. It's a very good family."

"And Samuel and I are engaged," Nonnie said. "I had planned to return to India with Samuel to meet his mother and father. I have a ticket for the plane."

"How long has Samuel been gone?" Connie asked.

"Five days," Nonnie said. "He left for work, and he never returned. We asked his employer, and they said Samuel didn't show up that day. We came here because we saw the newspaper article, and we hoped Mr. Plum would be able to help us find Samuel."

"Have you checked Samuel's room to see if anything is missing?" I asked. "Clothes? Passport?"

"Everything is there."

"Have you reported his disappearance to the police?"

"We have not. Do you think we should do that?"

"*No,*" Connie said, voice just a tad too shrill, hitting Vinnie's cell phone number on her speed dial.

"We've got a situation here," Connie said to Vinnie. "Mrs. Apusenja is in the office. It seems Samuel Singh has gone missing."

At two in the morning when the weather is ideal and the lights are all perfectly timed, it takes twenty minutes to drive from the police station to the bail bonds office. Today, at two in the afternoon, under an overcast sky, Vinnie made the run in twelve minutes.

Ranger, Vinnie's top gun, had ambled in a couple minutes earlier at Vinnie's request. He was dressed in his usual black. His dark brown hair was pulled back from his face and tied into a short ponytail at the nape of his neck. His short jacket looked suspiciously like Kevlar, and I knew from experience it hid a Glock. Ranger was always armed. And Ranger was always dangerous. His age was somewhere between twenty-five and thirty-five, and his skin was the color of a mocha latte. The story goes that Ranger had been special forces before signing on with Vinnie to do bond enforcement. He had a lot of muscle and a skill level somewhere between Batman and Rambo.

A while ago Ranger and I spent the night together. We were in an uneasy alliance now, working as a team when necessary, avoiding contact or conversation that would lead to a repeat sexual encounter. At least *I* was avoiding a repeat encounter. Ranger was his usual silent, mysterious self, his thoughts unknown, his attitude provocative. He'd chosen a chair that put his back to the wall. He sat relaxed and watchful, only his eyes moving when Vinnie came in like gangbusters.

"Talk to me," Vinnie said to Connie.

"Not much to tell. This is Mrs. Apusenja and her daughter Nonnie. Samuel Singh rented a room in the Apusenja house. They haven't seen him in five days."

"Christ," Vinnie said. "National print coverage on this. A week to go. And this sonnovabitch goes missing. Why didn't he just come over to my house and feed me rat poison? It would have been less painful."

"We think there might be foul play involved," Nonnie said.

Vinnie made a half-hearted effort to squash a grimace. "Yeah, right. Give me a refresher course on Samuel Singh. What was his normal routine?" Vinnie had the file in his hand, flipping pages, mumbling as he read. "It says here he worked at TriBro Tech. He was in the quality control department."

"During the week, Samuel would be at work from seven-thirty to five. Every night, he would stay home and watch television. On the weekends, he would help us run errands, and sometimes we would go to a movie," Nonnie said.

"Did he have friends? Relatives in the area?" Vinnie asked.

"There were people at his workplace that he spoke of, but he did not see them when the workday was over."

"Did he have enemies? Debts?"

Nonnie shook her head no. "He was a good man. Everyone liked him."

"Drugs?" Vinnie asked.

"No. And he drank alcohol only on special occasions."

"How about criminal activity? Was he involved with anyone shady?"

"Certainly not."

Ranger was impassive in his corner, watching the women. Nonnie was leaning forward in her chair, animated, worried. Mama Apusenja had her lips pressed tight together, her hands still tightly clasped in her lap.

"Anything else?" Vinnie asked.

Nonnie fidgeted in her seat. Her eyes dropped to the purse in her lap. "My little dog," Nonnie finally said. "My little dog is missing." She opened her purse and extracted a photo. "His name is Boo because he is so white. Like a ghost. He disappeared the day after Samuel vanished. He was in the backyard, which is fenced, and he disappeared."

We all looked at the photo of Nonnie and Boo. Boo was a small Cockapoo with black button eyes in a fluffy white face.

"Do you get along okay with your neighbors?" Vinnie asked. "Have you asked any of them if they've seen the dog?"

"No one has seen Boo."

"We must leave now," Mrs. Apusenja said, glancing at her watch. "Nonnie needs to get back to work."

Vinnie saw them to the door and watched them cross the street to their car. "There they go," Vinnie said. "Hell's message bearers." He shook his head. "I was having such a good day. Everyone was saying how good I looked in the picture. Everyone was congratulating me because I was doing something about visa enforcement. Okay, so I took a few comments when I dragged a naked, greased-up, fat guy into the station, but I could handle that." He gave his head another shake. "*This* I can't handle. This has to get fixed. I can't afford to lose this guy. Either we find this guy, dead or alive, or we're all unemployed. If I can't enforce this visa bond after all the publicity, I'm going to have to change my name, move to Scottsdale, Arizona, and sell used cars." Vinnie focused on Ranger. "You can find him, right?"

The corners of Ranger's mouth tipped up a fraction of an inch. This was the Ranger equivalent to a smile.

"I'm gonna take that as a *yes*," Vinnie said.

"I'll need help," Ranger told him.

"Fine. Whatever. You can have Stephanie."

Ranger cut his eyes to me and the smile widened ever so slightly—the sort of smile you see on a man when he's presented with an unexpected piece of pie.

Introducing the first ever "Plumography"— your guide to the world of all things Plum!

"There are some men who enter a woman's life and screw it up forever. Joseph Morelli did this to me—not forever, but periodically."

ONE FOR THE MONEY

Meet Stephanie Plum. The Trenton native just got laid off as discount lingerie buyer for E.E. Martin's in Newark, but the worst part is, she lost her cherished Mazda Miata to the repo man. Replacement: a used Nova with a bad muffler. A visit to her parents and her Grandma Mazur, who lives with them, leads to a light at the end of the Jersey Tunnel: a job with her cousin Vinnie at Vincent Plum Bail Bonding Company. Ten thousand a pop for hauling in the bad guys—guys like Joe Morelli, Stephanie's childhood nemesis-turned-hunky-vice-cop now wanted on a murder rap. Still as sexy and dangerous as ever, the heat is on—and working with just-as-hot fellow bondsman and mentor, Ranger, Stephanie could get burned. The bright side? Stephanie's junked her Nova and hijacked Morelli's Jeep Cherokee. Unfortunately, it's soon blown to smithereens. Packing pepper spray and a .38 Special, and with two new men in her life, it looks like a promising new career for Stephanie Plum . . .

"Morelli and I had done battle before. With only short-lived victories on both sides, I suspected this would be another war of sorts. And I figured I'd have to learn to live with it."

TWO FOR THE DOUGH

Stephanie Plum is trying to ease into her new job with a level head. It appears Joe Morelli is around for good—and bad—and she's resigned to it. Her loose professional relationship with Ranger ends in a platonic night together with no strings attached, and her new set of wheels, a secondhand Jeep Wrangler, suits her needs. Until it's stolen out from under her. How is she supposed to nab Kenny Mancuso, her new bail jumper and a distant relative of Morelli's? In a burst of misguided good intentions, she's strong-armed into accepting as a gift a 1953 Buick passed down from Grandma Mazur's brother, Sandor. It may look like a beluga whale but it's a car built to last—much to Stephanie's chagrin. Meanwhile, Morelli, whose libido has been stuck on overdrive ever since he met Stephanie years ago, is ready to make the moves on the resistant bounty hunter. Will she cave? Not on her Grandma's life—which happens to be in danger from an ice pick–wielding goon . . .

"I wasn't sure why I was still working for Vinnie. I suspected it had something to do with the title. Bounty hunter. It held a certain cachet. Even better, the job didn't require panty hose."

THREE TO GET DEADLY

Uncle Mo Bedemier may have a reputation as a kindly old candy-store owner but all that changes when he skips bail on a very minor charge. Bounty hunter Stephanie Plum needs to know why and that means scouting Uncle Mo's neighborhood. And no one knows Stark Street better than the new file clerk, Lula, a former hooker with an attitude—and better yet, a Nissan in working order. This seamier side of Jersey is where Stephanie comes to after a knock on the head, a corpse at her heels, and Joe Morelli on her tail as the possible murderer. Before the investigation is over, Ranger loses his Beemer, no thanks to Stephanie; the Nissan ends up in the shop for repairs; and Stephanie winds up with a green Mazda as loaner and red highlights in her hair. It certainly gets Morelli's attention because it prompts a first kiss on the back of Stephanie's very vulnerable neck . . .

"From here on out, Morelli was erotica non grata. *'Look but Don't Touch,' that was my motto."*

FOUR TO SCORE

It's been months since Joe Morelli made his move on Stephanie Plum, and true to form, it's been months since she's heard from him again. But the minute he returns, the rugged vice cop again proves irresistible—for at least one more night. She'd kick herself for giving in if she wasn't so preoccupied with a bail jumper: a waitress on the run for stealing her boyfriend's car. To make matters even worse, Vinnie's hired Joyce Barnhardt, Stephanie's high school rival and eventual home-wrecker, to join the bounty-hunting team as a skip tracer. Now, with the help of Lula riding shotgun in Stephanie's new Honda CRX, and a transvestite named Sally Sweet, Stephanie becomes embroiled in a game of murder, extortion, and kidnapping. Where it all leads is back into Morelli's arms—wrapped up on a motorcycle powered with 109 horses taking her to places she'd promised she'd never go again.

"When I was a little girl I used to dress Barbie up without underpants . . . And being a bail enforcement agent is sort of like being a bare-bottom Barbie. It's about having a secret."

HIGH FIVE

With her Honda CRX now just a memory of blown-up cinders, Stephanie's back in her '53 Buick—a "classic", she defends, with *no* authority. But with absolute conviction she's on the hunt for a vanishing relative. According to Grandma Mazur, Uncle Fred's gone missing. Seventy years old, just left the bank, and an easy mark. It doesn't look good. Whatever link the disappearance has to the rough beating of her friend, Lula, Stephanie's determined to find it. By way of a Porsche, garbage truck, and a BMW, past a nasty, vertically-challenged bookie and a stun-gun-toting Grandma Mazur, and through a Mafia wedding, Stephanie's bound and determined to make it out alive. But whether she ends up with Ranger or Morelli—both of whom make their intentions known—is a fate that she leaves to the heavens . . . and a simple draw of the name.

"Two of the men on my list of desirables actually desire me back. The problem being that they both sort of scare the hell out of me."

HOT SIX

Stephanie Plum's career as a bounty hunter may finally be taking its toll—on both her used Civic Honda and her emotions. Ranger has just been arrested by a rookie cop on a concealed weapons charge. Simple enough, until Ranger disappears. It seems he's also wanted in connection with the murder of a gun-trader's son. Now Stephanie wants Ranger in the worst way while Joe Morelli wants Stephanie in the *best* way. But Joe's private time is cramped by Grandma Mazur who moves in with Stephanie for the forseeable future. That's not the only surprise Grandma has: a suitor, Eddie DeChooch, hints at an exquisite night of sin. Stephanie's not so lucky. After her car is torched, she ends up with a one-of-a-kind Rollswagon that's drawing stares, and a sideline as a dog-sitter. But her biggest concern—next to finding Ranger—is Grandma Mazur's bid for a driver's license. With the streets endangered and Stephanie's life turned upside down, Morelli offers what he can to help. To Stephanie's surprise it's a proposal of marriage . . .

"Morelli's still trouble . . . but now he's the kind of trouble a woman likes."

SEVEN UP

Joe Morelli? Marriage? Sharing a bathroom? He must be desperate. But is Stephanie? At least, desperate to put her new bounty hunt to rest, anyway. After getting caught smuggling a truckload of bootleg cigarettes up from Virginia, Eddie DeChooch missed his court date. Stephanie doesn't want to have anything to do with it. After all, Eddie not only left behind a bullet-riddled corpse in his garden, but he's dating her Grandma Mazur. It's all hitting a little too close to home—so does the bombshell news leveled by Stephanie's sister, Valerie: a marriage break-up that's brought the depressed wife back to her roots. While Stephanie's considering her own marriage to Morelli, two of her childhood friends vanish. For answers she turns to the only man who can help. Ranger's deal? He'll give Stephanie everything she needs—if she gives him everything he wants. Trouble is, what he wants, Stephanie wants just as bad! With divided attention between the two men in her life, Stephanie finally relents, and grants Ranger his wish, leaving Morelli behind. How big a mistake could it be? She's about to find out . . .

"A few months ago Ranger and I made a deal that has haunted me—another one of those jumping off the garage roof things, except this deal involved my bedroom . . ."

HARD EIGHT

Stephanie Plum is on the hunt for a mother and child on the run who have left behind an angry ex-husband. He's eager to collect on a child custody bond. When local thug and businessman Eddie Abruzzi warns Stephanie to lay off of the case, she's only more intrigued. And a little scared, especially when she finds a bag of snakes on her doorknob and tarantulas in her car. What Stephanie needs is back-up, and Ranger's more than available—for the bounty hunt, and for Stephanie. Soon, a stalker in a bunny suit is on Stephanie's tail, her CRV is blown to bits, and a corpse winds up on her couch. That's just one body too many in Stephanie's house, considering her Grandma Mazur and sister, Valerie, have moved in, leaving little room for Joe Morelli who wants back into Stephanie's life. Before the case closes, she's sure to find her man. It's the other two men Stephanie has to contend with that are putting the perplexed and love-sick bounty hunter's heart at risk . . .